CAT IS BACK
AT BAT

by John Stadler

DUTTON CHILDREN'S BOOKS
NEW YORK

Library of Congress Cataloging-in-Publication Data

Stadler, John.
  Cat is back at bat / by John Stadler.
    p. cm.
  Summary: Fourteen rhymed verses describe unusual activities
of animals. Examples: "A big pig tries a wig." and "A snake
tries to bake a cake."
  ISBN 0-525-44762-8
  [1. Animals—Fiction. 2. Stories in rhyme.] I. Title.
PZ7.S77575Cat 1991
[E]—dc20   90-24831 CIP AC

Published in the United States by
Dutton Children's Books,
a division of Penguin Books USA Inc.

Printed in Hong Kong
First Edition   10 9 8 7 6 5 4 3 2

For Nomi
From Dahomey

The cat

is back

at bat.

An ape

in a cape

has a scrape.

A shark

hears a bark

in the park.

A raccoon

will soon

be on the moon.

A pup

in a cup

goes up.

A moose

and a goose

run loose.

A big

pig

wears a wig.

A snake

tries to bake

a cake.

A mouse

makes a blouse

for a house.

A chick

does a trick

with a brick.

A goat

in a coat

sails a boat.

A fat

rat

wears a hat.

A crab

tries to grab

a cab.

A toad

in the road

carries a load.